A SHORT HISTORY
OF HOW YOU COME TO BE READING MY
VERY PRIVATE DIARIES

In a snail shell, they were STOLEN. Oh yes, no less. My witch Haggy Aggy (HA for short) sneaked into my log basket and helped herself.

According to her, this is what happened:

On one of her many shopping trips to Your Side she met a Book Wiz. (I am told you call them publishers, though Wiz seems more fitting as they make books appear, as if by magic, <u>every day of the week</u>.)

Anyway, this Book Wiz/publisher wanted HA to write an account of HER life as a witch here on Our Side. Of course, HA wasn't willing to do <u>that</u>. Being the most unwilling witch in witchdom, she is far too busy shopping, watching telly, not cackling, being anything BUT a witch and getting me into trouble with the High Hags* as a result.

The Book Wiz begged on her knees (apparently) and offered HA a life's supply of shoes if she came up with something. So HA did. She came up with THIS — MY DIARIES. ALL OF THEM!!!!

Of course, when I wrote the diaries, I was <u>not</u> expecting anyone to read them. Let alone Othersiders like you. But as you are, here is a word to the wise about how things work between us:

---

* The High Hags run everything round here. They RULE.

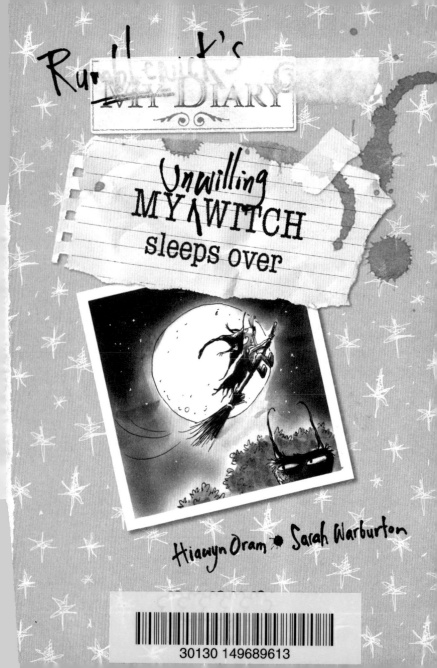

Ru~~mblewick's~~
~~MY~~ DIARY

Unwilling
MY∧WITCH
sleeps over

Hiawyn Oram • Sarah Warburton

1. We are here on THIS SIDE and you are there on the OTHER SIDE.

2. Between us is the HORIZON LINE.

3. You don't see we're here, on This Side, living our lives, because for you the HORIZON LINE is <u>always</u> <u>a day away</u>. You can walk for a thousand moons (or more for all I know), but you'll never reach it.

4. On the other paw, we know you're there because we visit you all the time. This is partly because of broomsticks. A broomstick has no trouble with any Horizon Line anywhere. A broomstick (with one or more of us upon it) just flies straight through.

And it has to be like that because scaring Otherside children into their wits is part of witches' work. In fact it is Number One on the Witches' Charter of Good Practice (see copy glued at the back).

On the other paw, it is NOWHERE in the Charter for a witch to go over to Your Side to make friends and try to be and do everything you are and do — <u>as my witch Haggy Aggy does</u>.

But then, that's my giant problem: being cat to a witch who doesn't want to be one. And as you will see from these diaries, it makes my life a right BAG OF HEDGEHOGS. So all I can say is, if HA tries to make friends with YOU, send her straight back to This Side with a spider in her ear.

Thank you,

Rumblewick Spellwacker Mortimer B. xxx

THIS DIARY BELONGS TO:

Rumblewick Spellwacker Mortimer B.

RUMBLEWICK for short, RB for shortest

ADDRESS:
Thirteen Chimneys,
Wizton-under-Wold, This Side
Bird's Eye View: 331 N by WW

TELEPHONE:
77+3-5+1-7

NEAREST OTHERSIDE TELEPHONE:
Ditch and Candleberry Bush Street,
N by SE Over the Horizon

BIRTH DAY:
Windy Day 23rd Magogary

Education:
The Awethunder School For Familiars
12-Moon Apprenticeship to the
High Hag Witch Trixie Fiddlestick

Qualifications:
Certified Witch's Familiar

Current Employment:
Seven-year contract with Witch Hagatha Agatha,
Haggy Aggy for short, HA for shortest

Hobbies:
Catnastics, Point-to-Point Shrewing, Languages

Next of Kin:
Uncle Sherbet (retired Witch's Familiar)
Mouldy Old Cottage,
Flying Teapot Street,
Prancetown

Foggy Night In The Far Quagmires

Dear Diary,

Sorry if this looks skew-wiggle. We're sleeping over at Haggy Aggy's aunt's in the Far Quagmires — and I'm writing under the spare bed, by the light of a tired firefly.

We only came for our usual once-a-moon drop-in. But then the fog came down and Pondernot (HA's aunt) wouldn't let us fly home in it.

Haggy Aggy is in the bed, tossing and turning so hard, she's sending the mattress straw flying— all over me and all over you. I'm certain she's sleeping so badly on purpose — as a protest — because she doesn't want to be here.

And I can sympathise with that.

7

Pondernot is a bent little
witch with rosy cheeks.

To look at her you'd think she
couldn't bring a brew to a bubble in
a boiling cauldron.

But one thing is certainly boiling about
her: only she, in the whole universe,
is able to make HA feel RUBBLEROT
about not being a more willing witch.

And this visit,
thanks to her
snooping Familiar

— Sassy
Elevenlives
Selfright —

there's been more
than usual to
make HA feel
RUBBLEROT about.

Apparently last Ghastly night, Sassy the Snoop 'just happened' to drop in to the Deep Ditch in Wizton — a favourite Familiars' haunt.

While she was there, it 'just happened' that the High Hags' Familiars came in.

(Well, surprise, surprise, as everyone knows they always go to the Deep Ditch on Ghastly night.)

9

It also 'just happened' that their
tattlechat was all about HA and how their
Hags suspect she's trying to become less of
a witch and more of an Othersider with
every moon that passes.

I can imagine the Snoop couldn't get
home fast enough to tell Pondernot.
And, furnished with this information,
Pondernot has been making HA feel like
complete GRUBSPIT.

Not by harrying and pointing her pointing finger. She never does that. But by getting under HA's skin with sharp little needles of 'deep disappointment'. Somehow making HA feel GUILTY for getting HER a bad reputation by association.

Now, while on the one paw,
I wish I had Pondernot's ability to do
this, on the other I'm glad I do not.

For one good reason: feeling
guilty does not suit Haggy Aggy.
It puts her in a mood so dark it's as if
she's under a personal eclipse of the sun
and moon and can't see her own foot
in front of her.

Back at Thirteen Chimneys After Getting Lost and Diverted By The JIM

Dear Diary,

We're home, thank the stars. Back from the Far Quagmires, though by no means out of the 'quagmire'.

To continue: what with the grubspit feelings of guilt and having to sleep over — by the time the fog lifted and we came to leave Pondernot's — HA's mood was so dark she could hardly see her way out of the front door.

Though I was standing there ready with our broomstick, she walked straight past me and nearly fell into one of the bog fires in what Pondernot fondly calls her

'garden'.

This put her into
an even fouler mood.

Followed by an even fouler one,
when Pondernot said with a crooked
smile, "Now my dear, you know
how much it would upset me to see
a fully-fledged witch being flown by
her Familiar. So I hope you'll be flying
that broomstick home yourself as any
AUNT-RESPECTING witch would do."

With a thundery snarl, HA grabbed
our broomstick, mounted it and
took off with barely time for
me to leap on behind.

Well, the truth is, Diary, in the dark mood she was in, HA should <u>NOT</u> have been flying anything, anywhere. Let alone from the Far Quagmires to Wizton-Under-Wold. It requires much alertness of the stars above and landmarks below. It should <u>NEVER</u> be attempted by one in a personal eclipse and hardly able to see

her own flying hand

in front of her.

So, inevitably, inspite of my attempts to navigate from the back of the broom,

WE WENT THE WRONG WAY.

We went so wrong, we ended up crossing the Horizon and flying uselessly hither and thither on the Other Side, until HA said she was feeling so sick she was going to fall off.

I took my life in my paws, clung and clawed my way past her to take over the flying, and quickly brought us down — as I thought safely — on

the nearest
suitable landing place.

As it turned out — it wasn't safe or suitable.

It was the roof of a building in which, HA was soon to discover, Otherside children go to do JIM (similar to cathastics, if a clumsier version).

And now that we were off-broomstick and away from guilt and the Far Quagmires, HA's dark mood suddenly lifted.

Her sun and moon came out again.

She dangled cheerfully from the water-pipes of the building, so she could peer in and eavesdrop at a half-open window.

"Oh RB," she cried, "do take a look.

There are darling girls in there doing what they call JIM — leaping, tumbling, propelling and turning free through the air. No springs on their feet, no wings on their shoulders! Oh, how I'd love to be what they be and do what they do. And do you know what? Because I would love to,

I've decided _I will!_"

Well, you know
Haggy Aggy.
Once she's
decided, she's decided.
So forget Pondernot's
guiltifyings about being more
Other Side than This Side.

An Otherside JIM girl
is what HA
is going to <u>be</u>!!

21

I mean, we've only been home five tads of tell and she's already turned herself into a JIM Girl Lookalike.

And magicked up a 'JIM' bag full of 'JIM' wear so tomorrow she can join the 'darling JIM girls' in their JIMMY activities.

She is in her room now, trying out a spell she made me invent the moment we came in the door — namely

The Triple-Turn-in-Air-
-Without-Landing-in-
a-Complete-Splat spell.

I don't know how but I've got to keep this from the tattlechat at the Deep Ditch.

Imagine if Sassy the Snoop hears of it and informs Aunt Pondernot?

All I can say is, dark moodwise,

better not ponder it!

JIM Day the First Night

Dear Diary,

Talk about being exhausted. I've had to spend all afternoon in that JIM building tucked down in HA's JIM bag,

'OBSERVING AND LEARNING
SO AS TO HELP HER
BECOME A GREAT JIMMER'.

And then, since we got home, I've had to invent four more spells, 'using what I've observed and learnt.'

<u>All</u>, please note, when I was supposed to be somewhere quite else — at practice for

the Grand Steeple Chase Race!!

25

More of that later.

For now, here are all five spells (which she's asked me to set in a booklet she can tuck it into her JIM pants for easy reference).

Spell 1

THE TRIPLE-TURN-IN-AIR-
WITHOUT-FEAR-OF-
GOING-SPLAT SPELL

Tuck yourself up tight as a catkin
bud in a witch's hat and chant:

My feet are sprung like springy springs
My feet so sprung will give me wings
And stepping from this witch's hat
I'll fly up from the gymnast's mat
And in a wondrous sky-high bound
I'll have the time to turn me round
Not once, not twice but three times over
Then land as if I land in CLOVER.

THE FLY-OVER-
THE-HORSE SPELL

Make your broomstick invisible using any
reliable Invisible Broomstick spell.
Lie on 'the horse' and chant with authority:

You are no longer lifeless
You are a living horse
As vaulting you I must be
You'll help me in my course
And as I come a-flying
You'll be there for my hands
While making very, very sure
You're NOT there when I lands.

THE GLUED-ON-A-BEAM SPELL

Mix one dollop spider's web jam, one dollop burr jelly, one dollop pine tree goo. Just before you mount the balance beam, apply mixture to soles of your shoes or feet and chant:

I will stay, I will stick
I will never stumble
See my feet return so neat
From each leap and tumble
I'm so stable, I'm so able
I can make the team
I am glued on like I'm screwed on —
TO THIS BALANCE BEAM.

THE NO-HANDS-SWING-BARS SPELL

When called to mount the bars, twirl on your left foot backwards seven times while chanting inwardly:

I am so sure between these bars
I circle, swing, release
It seems I am a Spinning Wheel
My speed I don't decrease.
I am supreme between these bars
I hardly need them there
One giant swing and look — no hands — I am at home in air.

Spell [5]

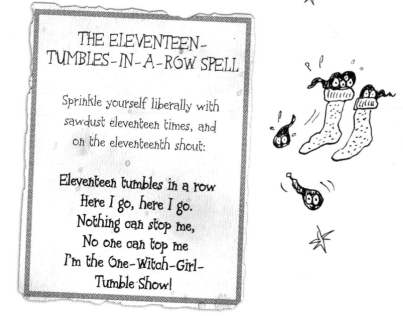

THE ELEVENTEEN-TUMBLES-IN-A-ROW SPELL

Sprinkle yourself liberally with sawdust eleventeen times, and on the eleventeenth shout:

Eleventeen tumbles in a row
Here I go, here I go.
Nothing can stop me,
No one can top me
I'm the One-Witch-Girl-Tumble Show!

Not bad, given I've only been acquainted with JIM for **SOCKS, SOCKS,**

TADPOLES IN SOCKS!

What's going on. The whole house is shaking. Is it the end of the universe? Be back when I've found out ~~~~

Dear Diary,

Sorry to keep you in suspense. It wasn't the end of the universe or even Wizton-Under-Wold.

Apparently, at JIM, HA made friends with two JIM GIRLS named Zinnea and Tulip. They've invited her for a shake at a nearby Shake Bar after jimming tomorrow.

<u>So</u>, because HA always has to be the best at everything (except being a proper witch), she has been practising her shake.

Well, I hope they don't invite her every day.

I mean look at this place? I'll be working till dawn unshaking it.

HA Gets An Even Worse
Invitation Day Night

Dear Diary

Can you believe this? HA got it all wrong. A Shake Bar is not a place you go to shake yourself till the universe trembles. It is a kind of Gatheria where you meet with your friends — to slurp googuff through hollow reeds — called straws.

When HA discovered this, she picked up her JIM bag (me in it) and rushed to the Shake Bar washroom. Here, she had the nerve to give me an ear-wigging!

"Why didn't you <u>TELL</u> me a shake is a drink?" she hissed as she wigged one ear.

"Because I had no idea!" I hissed back.

"Well, why didn't you? You're my Familiar. You're supposed to be Othersidewise,"

she wigged the

other ear.

Luckily
Zinnea came in at
that moment and asked
her who she was talking to
in a locked flush-it-away
booth — which ended the wigging before
my ears were completely wigged off.

Mind you, getting a wigging in
a washroom turned out to be the
least of my worries.

While HA and the girls were slurping
(after the wigging) this is what I heard
(from the JIM bag):

It was the Tulip girl. "Aggy," she said,
"as it's Saturday, Zin's allowed to sleep
over at mine tonight. D'you
want to come too?"

Well, I nearly jumped out of the bag
onto Tulip's lap to tell her

NO, UNDER NO CIRCUMSTANCES

CAN 'AGGY' SLEEP ANYWHERE TONIGHT.

IT IS THE HEATS OF

THE WITCH'S CAT STEEPLE CHASE AND

SHE HAS TO BE THERE TO WARRANT FOR

ME OR I WILL NOT BE ALLOWED

TO ENTER!

Somehow I held myself back, only to hear HA say in a cooey voice:

"Oh, Tulip,
that is SWEET of you.

Normally I don't like sleeping over.

But if you mean wearing

a pink nightdress and watching TV

all night on your sofa,

then I should think so!"

At this Zinnea giggled and Tulip said, "Yes, though Zin and I wear jimjams. They're better for bouncing in. And don't forget your toothbrush because my mum makes us clean our teeth, even though she knows we have a midnight feast afterwards.

So if you want to come, here's my address."

Well, when we left that Shake Bar, HA started screeching with excitement.

"I'm going to **sleep over!**

With Zin and Tu!

And meet a MUM.

And be told to brush my teeth

before a midnight feast!

Oh I'm so excited, I could fly!"

I was SO embarrassed — there were passers by — but there was no time for that. I had to get her home triple presto and talk some sense into her head about the importance of the Steeple Chase Heats.

I mean. I've been training for this race for moons. I'm GOOD at Steeple Chasing. THE BEST.

Oh no... I'll have to go. HA is calling me to help her work out what JIMJAMS are.

From which you can deduce that so far
I haven't persuaded her not to sleep over at
Tulip's house. Though I haven't given up
hope that I will.

THE BEST
STEEPLE
CHASER

RUMBLEWICK

Dear Diary,

Sadly, I have to report the following:
HA DID go to sleep over with 'Tu and Zin'
and I DIDN'T get to enter the Heats because
she WASN'T there to warrant that I hadn't
used any magic to make me fly faster.

This is how it went:

I BEGGED

on all fours

for her to attend.

She wasn't interested. "Oh, RB, borrow someone else's witch. Like that old frog-brewer next door..."

"She can't," I protested, "she's entering Grimey. And a witch can only warrant for one cat."

"Then find a witch who isn't entering a cat and ask her," HA said. "Anyway, being invited to sleep over at Tu's is the best thing that's ever happened to me and if you care about me, you won't spoil it."

With that,
she was off in her
pink car,

in her JIM wear under
a jam-coloured nightdress
(the best we could come up
with for jimjams)
and carrying a tooth scrubber
of finest elm twigs.

Of course, I should have gone after her.
And de-activated the fly-mode on that car
before she crossed the Horizon.

But I wasn't ready to give up on the
Steeple Chase. I fetched my best racing
broomstick and flew to the Clearing
where the Heats start, in the tad of hope
that there was a spare witch
who'd warrant for me.

It was while I was asking around if anyone knew of one that Grimey came rushing up.

"RB, I've been trying to find you to tell you. I was in the Deep Ditch last Ghastly night when the Hags' Familiars were tattlechatting about Haggy Aggy being more Other Side than This Side."

"Tell me something new," I sighed.

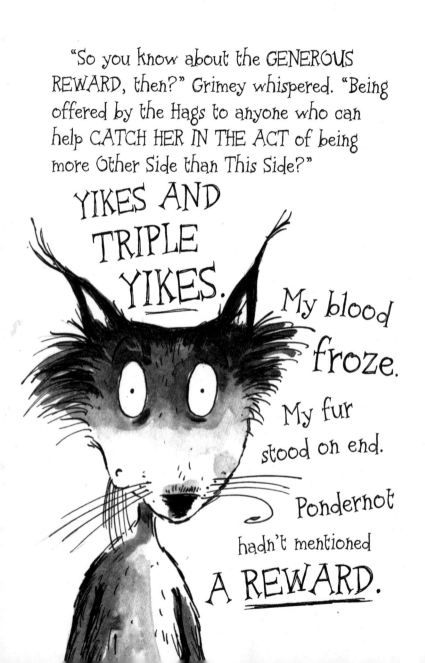

"So you know about the GENEROUS REWARD, then?" Grimey whispered. "Being offered by the Hags to anyone who can help CATCH HER IN THE ACT of being more Other Side than This Side?"

YIKES AND TRIPLE YIKES.

My blood froze.

My fur stood on end.

Pondernot hadn't mentioned A REWARD.

And I could guess why. She didn't know — because Sassy the Snoop, hadn't told her.

She's kept that part of the tattlechat to herself because she wants to be the one who catches HA and claims the

'REWARD!!'

WANTED

HAGGY AGGY

GENEROUS REWARD OFFERED

TO HELP CATCH HER IN THE ACT OF BEING MORE OTHER SIDE THAN THIS SIDE

H.O.H.

Well, how I had a GIANT problem on my paws, didn't I?

I muttered thanks for the info to Grimey and wished him luck in the Heats.

"You too," he said.

Before I could explain I wouldn't be taking part, Sassy appeared at my side.

"Rumblewick, hello again!" she sniggered. "Aren't you entering? Or is your witch too busy — somewhere else — to be here and warrant for you?"

It was a case of
SAYING ANYTHING to put her
in her place, so I said, "No,
Sassy Selfright, she's working on

a new collection of

New Moon spells.

Working so hard
she's too busy
to be here."

And wished I hadn't.
Because in that tad of
trice Pondernot was beside
us AND SHE HEARD.
Her face lit up like
the evening star.

"Well, well! My Hagatha, working on a new collection of New Moon spells? How thrillingly willing! How richly witchly! Now, we must make sure the High Hags hear about THIS."

"No!" I squealed like a trapped rat. "No one must know. It's still work-in-secret."

"Oh, but she wouldn't mind me, her dear aunt, having a little preview?" said Pondernot. "It would so lift my spirit to find her reforming in the matter of spell-making and witchly willingness."

So I got tough. I said, glaring mostly at Sassy, "If ANYONE comes snooping before she's ready, HA has told me she will burn the WHOLE COLLECTION."

Tell you more later. HA's come in from her sleepover and she's yelling for me!

HA Bubbles Over And The Snoop Comes Snooping

Dear Diary,

Well, in she breezed, kicking off her shoes and bubbling over with excitement.

Of course, first she had to blame me for what HADN'T gone right: why hadn't I told her when you go to a sleepover you don't GO in your sleepover wear? Why hadn't I told her JIM-age girls DON'T DRIVE CARS? Why didn't I tell her that a Mum is only a kind of High Hag but nicer who tells you to go to bed when you want to stay up watching TV?

And why did I give her **twigs** to clean her teeth and not a BRUSH?

But when she'd got all that out, she whipped off her nightdress — revealing herself in a pair of striped pantlets and the shortest dress surely ever made — and became sweetness and light.

"Whatever RB, I forgive you because I had such a superhova time. And look! These are jimjams!"

She twirled round, jumped onto the sofa and started bouncing on it as she spoke, "Tu gave them to me because I didn't have any and she has seven pairs! Oh, and I learned to giggle which is SO all that. And to bounce on a bed like this a hundred and one times without falling off. And as for sleepover food! You HAVE to taste peanut butter at midnight. AND do you know what? Tu, Zin and me are now so close we're like THIS!"

She twined two fingers round each other and held them up. "And because we're like <u>THIS</u>, I'm invited to sleep over

EVERY
Saturday
until the end
of <u>ever!</u>"

Well, it was another
YIKES AND TRIPLE YIKES moment.
What did she mean 'every Saturday
night till the end of ever?' Had she gone
bats on a broomstick in a burning belfry?

I was just considering the kindest way to
tell her she couldn't go sleeping over on the
Other Side AT ALL because the Hags were
after her, when what caught my eye
through the window?

Sassy — on a broomstick — flying
past our house.

Then flying past again and and
landing behind the Candleberry Bushes!!

So, the Snoop _had_
come snooping.

To try and catch

HAGGY AGGY

OUT.

There wasn't a tad
of tell to
waste. I had
to make a plan,
triple presto.

My Brilliant Plan

Dear Diary,

I put a plan together

fast enough,

I can tell you.

First I closed the curtains and blocked up all of our thirteen chimneys.

Then I got HA to go to bed — which wasn't hard as, apparently, she hadn't slept a wink at the sleepover.

While she slept, I wrote a note to Tu and Zin in Otherside handwriting which thankfully I learnt so well at school.

Here is a copy:

Dear Tu and Zin

For your information Aggy is not what she seems. She is not a girl jimmer. She is A WITCH. A true and proper witch even if she doesn't always behave like one. Believe me, I am a highly trained Witch's Familiar and I know.

So if you are horrified — which you should be — and do not want a witch in your JIM class or at your sleepovers, my advice is BANISH HER

AT THE FIRST OPPORTUNITY.

Yours truly,

I'd better not give my name.

<u>PS</u>: If you don't believe me take a look in your garden. All the witch's artefacts you find there are HERS.

<u>PPS</u>: It will be best if you do not tell her you received this warning. Just say 'you guessed' because of her supernova JIM — which, by the way, has all been mightily spelled.

Next I filled two large ingredient collecting bags with the following:

One fold-away broomstick
One porta-cauldron
One full witch's all-black
outfit including hat
Three jars of allspell ingredients
— dried slug slime, blagwort
seeds, weasel earwax.

With the bags astraddle my broomstick — and the Note safely tucked under my hat — I flew off towards the Tanglewoods which are well-known collecting grounds. So if Sassy was watching from behind the Candleberry Bushes, she wouldn't think I was up to anything unusual.

Once I was sure she wasn't following me, I changed direction and sped back over the Horizon to Tu's house. (Luckily I'd found her address under H.A's pillow.)

Here I placed the contents of my bags in a convenient garden shed and pushed THE NOTE through Tu's bedroom window.

To be sure she got the message, I waited and watched until I saw her pick it up and read it!

Now all I had to do was get H.A to one last JIM class — where SURELY Tu would say, "ZIN and I DO NOT want a WITCH for a BEST FRIEND or bouncing with us on our very own beds in our very own houses. SO GO HOME, WITCH, AND STAY THERE."

And that would be the end of that. There'd be no more Otherside sleeping over for Sassy to catch her at!!

Brilliant, though I keep saying it myself.

Dear Diary,

As I arrived home, I saw Sassy in the bushes covered in chimney soot!! Good — I thought — try all thirteen chimneys. You won't get in that way. You won't get in any way. Because you won't be going any here. Especially, you won't be following HA to her last and all-important JIM class where — if everything goes according to my plan — she is going to be UNbefriended by her new, best, Otherside sleepover friends.

And so, the next day while HA was putting on her JIM wear, I grounded that selfrighting Snooper in the REAL sense of the word:

THE FAILPROOF-GROUNDING SPELL

Crush an old unflyable broomstick to dust and mix with pressed pine gum. Fly over the One To Be Grounded, sprinkling the mixture and chanting:

Wherever you wish to go
Wherever you wish to linger
You cannot move a foot
A paw or little finger
Wherever you wish to sneak
Whether it's near or far
The very ground you stand on
Holds you where you are!

SMALL PRINT: This spell is failproof unless the One Being Spelled uses a spell to override it within two tads of tell of it being performed on him/her/it.

And, as Sassy wasn't expecting it, she didn't have an overrider ready to override it. So there she was –

ACTUALLY STUCK IN THE MUD –

in her Snoop's hideout behind the

Candleberry Bushes!!!

My Brilliant Plan Backfires

Dear Diary,

So that the grounded Sassy wouldn't look up and see HA flying off in JIM wear, I offered to take her to the class myself — provided she COVER HERSELF UP in a cloak and hat.

I said there was a chill wind blowing and she wouldn't want to catch cold and not be at her best. She agreed without a fight, though with lots of moaning that I fuss too much.

Whatever, I didn't care. I was just relieved to deliver her to the door of the JIM building for what I felt certain was

THE BEGINNING OF THE END OF

OTHERSIDE SLEEPING OVER.

ONLY,

IT DID NOT
WORK OUT

LIKE THAT
AT ALL.

"RB," she crowed, as I picked her up afterwards, "Tu and Zin are SO EXCITED about having me for a best friend, they're asking all their other friends to the sleepover this Saturday night. To show me off! Now what am I going to WEAR for this SHOW-ME-OFF party?"

So excited?

About having A WITCH for a friend??

Talk about a plan backfiring.

I mean,

what were those

girls thinking of,

and now what???

The Grounding spell keeping Sassy stuck in the mud will have worn off by 'Saturday' night. She'll be on

A RAMPAGE OF REVENGE!!

(And no doubt ready with an overrider in case I try to ground her again!)

Besides — and it's a GIANT BESIDES — this 'Saturday' night is the night of the actual Steeple Chase Race.

Everyone will be there.

EVERY WITCH AND EVERY FAMILIAR.

If HA isn't, the High Hags will WANT TO KNOW WHERE SHE IS.

And if the Snoop follows HA to Tu's, which she will, she'll be able to lead the Hags straight to her.

HA will be caught in The Act and Sassy will claim the Reward.

And here's the thing, Diary —

SNOOPING will have won.

So I better get re-thinking because

I'M NOT HAVING THAT!

Dear Diary,

I thought and re-thought. The best I could come up with was to tell HA about the danger she was in.

But when I did she just brushed it all aside.

"Oh RB, let the Snoops snoop, let the Hags catch. Let them have their rewards. My reward — being shown-off at a sleepover — is far the greater!"

"But what about ME," I begged. "If you're caught at Tu's, _I'll_ get the blame for letting you go — and probably sent back to Awethunders to re-learn my lessons!"

"Oh, those old Hags are so full of hot soup," she laughed.

"They won't send you back to school —
there aren't enough Familiars to go round
as it is. So stop fretting!"

I shot my last arrow.

"Well, what about Pondernot? Think how
RUBBLEROT she's going to make you feel."

"She won't get the chance," HA laughed,
"as I'll NEVER drop in on her again!"

And that was that.

Haggy Aggy went to the sleepover.
Not even covered up in a cloak and hat.
Completely UNAWARE that Tu knows she is
a witch because her Familiar (YOURS
TRULY, ME) has told her. And with Sassy
the Snoop certain to be following her!!!

YIKES AND TRIPLE YIKES! I had to face
it: WHAT A GROTTLEPOTCH I WAS
MAKING OF THIS.

So after moping about for some tads of
tell, I decided I had no choice.

I had to go after HA on my own broomstick [1] to confess what I'd done and [2] to keep a look out for Sassy.

Several times as I flew I thought I saw her and went in hot pursuit — only to find I was chasing shadows.

As a result, by the time I arrived at Tu's — and took up my observation post in a tree — the sleepover was in full swing.

Though, of course, not at all as HA was expecting.

Tu, Zin and 'all their friends' were dragging her to the garden shed screaming,

"Come on, Aggy. Put on your witch's stuff. Show us how you ride a broomstick!"

"What do you mean?" HA gulped. "What witch's stuff? I am not a witch. What makes you think I am?"

"We guessed!" cried Zin. "From your JIM! Which is so magic you must be one!" They pushed her into the shed yelling,

"PUT IT ALL ON.
THEN RIDE YOUR BROOMSTICK.
WE LOVE WITCHES."

After a lot of thunderous snarling from inside, the shed door opened and HA emerged — in the black I'd put there and holding the broomstick.

"Ride, ride!"

cried Tulip.

"Show us how you do it."

HA turned green.

But she got astride the broomstick, shot up in the air, circled twice and landed proudly — without so much as a double foot brake.

Now Tu and Zin begged to be taken up for rides.

How could HA say 'no' to her best friends who were so close they were 'entwined'.

Looking even greener, she took them each up for a spin. Then, because the girl begged so hard, she took up one of the 'other friends'. And I could see exactly what she was trying to do.

Buck her off!

At the same tad of tell I saw something else I'd rather I hadn't: the unmistakable shape of a Familiar on a broom against the moon. Sassy!

My heart sank and then sank deeper when I realised the shape was heading AWAY from us.

She'd already been and seen and was no
doubt flying back to tell the Hags
where they could find HA being
shown off by Otherside
friends at an

Otherside
sleepover
party!!

Now what?
Go after her and
stop her?
Or save an unwitting

girl-child
from being

bucked off
a broomstick?

The girl started to fall. There was nothing for it. I swooped out and caught her neatly on the back of my broomstick.

But this only got me <u>more</u> into boil and bubble and no closer to going after Sassy.

HA was furious to find me there. Especially when the girls crowded round and made a huge fuss of <u>ME!</u>

"Thank you and enough," she snapped.

"I don't know who this cat is or w<u>ha</u>t it's doing here.

Let's watch TV."

"TV!?" cried Tulip. "Who wants to watch TV when there's a **real witch** and her **cat** to play with! And now we want you to make us a real spell."

Zin dragged the porta-cauldron out of the shed.

"Make us a spell to turn all the girls we don't like at school INTO SLIMY TOADS."

Tulip presented HA with a basket. "We've collected ingredients. All the horrid things you witches put in spells."

And suddenly I saw ALL WAS NOT LOST.

The basket was full of everything HA loves to protect: frogs, snails, a bat, a jar of newts and a terrified shrew.

Little did those girls know how the idea of using them would upset HA.

As they shrieked and demanded their spell, I could see a full-on witch's fit brewing.

"A spell!" she cried, going puce. "Using these dear living creatures? To turn girls you don't like into toads?

We'll see about that!!"

She grabbed the ingredients I'd put in the shed, flew up on her broomstick and sprinkled the girls with them, chanting:

Ghastly girls who are not kind
In this moment we will find
You're frogs and snails, <u>you're</u> bats, a shrew
Not living — that's too good for you
So wish you'd watched TV with me

FOR GARDEN
ORNAMENTS
<u>YOU BE!</u>

And — since she is a great witch when she's willing — immediately those girls were STONE.

Then yelling at me to join HER on her broomstick, she set off at the speed of lightness for This Side!!

And all I can say is: was our luck in or what?

We were just back over the Horizon when we met the Hags — being led by the Snoop and making for Tulip's — to catch HA IN THE ACT!

Instead, they
found us together on
a broomstick, as we should
be, HA flying it in top-to-toe black.

As they stopped, in surprise, I called out,
"Evening, Your Hagships. Going to the Other
Side, are you? Well, while there, go to
House Number 5, Partridge Close, and check
out one of Hagatha's New Moon spells. And
for your info, those garden ornaments were
all once GIRLS."

"And they will be again, when the spell
wears off," called HA, "only wiser for the
experience!"

The Hags spluttered — while Sassy went
into such a spin of disappointment, she
actually fell off her broomstick!! And HA
did the last thing I was expecting.

She called out: "Well, we can't hang about up here. We must get over to the Steeple Chase!"

And, knock me over with a dandelion, she added, "Oh and by the way, Amuletta. Rumblewick MUST be allowed to race even if he did miss the Heats.

And if you won't let him,

I'll turn you into a MUM!"

Well, clearly Amuletta didn't want to run that risk, because I did get to race.

And, as I am the best, I WAS the best and won — and have the trophy to prove it!!

Better still — Sassy didn't even make the race. When she fell off her broomstick, we were over the Tanglewoods. Of course, she wouldn't have come to any harm because — like name like nature — she could right herself even if she fell off the evening star.

But here's the thing: it takes almost a moon to walk it back to ANYWHERE from the Tanglewoods.

So all I can say to Sassy is — you got your just reward, Snoop

...AND KEEP WALKING!

WITCHES' CHARTER
OF GOOD PRACTICE

I. Scare at least one child on the **Other Side** into his or her wits – every day (excellent), once in seven days (good), once a moon (average), once in two moons (bad), once in a blue moon (failed).

2. Identify any fully-grown **Othersiders** who were not properly scared into their wits as children and **DO IT NOW**. (It is never too late for a grown Othersider to come to his or her senses.)

3. Invent a new spell useful for every purpose and every occasion in the **Witches' Calendar**. Ensure you or your Familiar commits it to a Spell Book before it is lost to the Realms of Forgetfulness for ever.

4. Keep a proper witch's house at all times – filled with dust and spiders' webs, mould and earwigs underthings and ensure the jars on your kitchen shelves are always alive with good spell ingredients.

5. Cackle a lot. Cackling can be heard far and wide and serves many purposes such as (i) alerting others to your terrifying presence (ii) sounding hideous and thereby comforting to your fellow witches.

6. Make sure your Familiar keeps your means of proper travel (broomsticks) in good trim and that one, either or both of you exercise them regularly.

7. Never fail to present yourself anywhere and everywhere in full witch's uniform (i.e. black everything and no ribbons upon your hat ever). Sleeping in uniform is recommended as a means of saving dressing time.

8. Keep your Familiar happy with a good supply of Comfrey and Slime Buns. Remember, behind every great witch is a well-fed Familiar.

9. At all times acknowledge the authority of your local High Hags. As their eyes can do 360 degrees and they know everything there is to know, it is always in your interests to make their wishes your commands.

CONTRACT OF SERVICE

between
WITCH HAGATHA AGATHA, Haggy Aggy for short, HA for shortest
of Thirteen Chimneys, Wizton-under-Wold
&
the Witch's Familiar,
RUMBLEWICK SPELLWACKER MORTIMER B, RB for short

It is hereby agreed that, come
FIRE, Brimstone, CAULDRONS overflowing
or ALIEN WIZARDS invading,
for the NEXT SEVEN YEARS
RB will serve HA,
obey her EVERY WHIM and WORD and at all times assist her
in the ways of being a true and proper WITCH.

PAYMENT for services will be:
* a log basket to sleep in   * unlimited Slime Buns for breakfast
* free use of HA's broomsticks (outside of peak brooming hours)
* and a cracked mirror for luck.

PENALTY for failing in his duties will be decided on the whim of
THE HAGS on HIGH.

SIGNED AND SEALED
this New Moon Day, 22nd of Remember

Haggy Aggy
....
Witch Hagatha Agatha

Rumblewick
....
Rumblewick Spellwacker Mortimer B

Trixie Fiddlestick
....
And witnessed by the High Hag, Trixie Fiddlestick

ORCHARD BOOKS

338 Euston Road, London NW1 3BH
Orchard Books Australia
Level 17/207 Kent Street, Sydney NSW 2000

ISBN: 978 I 84616 070 7

First published in 2007 by Orchard Books

A CIP catalogue record for this book is

available from the British Library.

Orchard Books is a division
of Hachette Children's Books

I 3 5 7 9 I0 8 6 4 2
Printed in China/Hong Kong

To Giselle and Nicola,
for being so
incredibly good
H.O.

For Lizzie
S.W.

Dear Precious Children

The Publisher asked me to say something about these Diaries.
(As I do not write Otherside very well, I have dictated it to
the Publisher's Familiar/assistant. If she has not written it
down right, let me know and I'll turn her into a fat pumpkin.)

This is my message: I went to a lot of trouble to steal these
Diaries for you. And the Publisher gave me a lot of shoes in
exchange. If you do not read them the Publisher may want the
shoes back. So please, for my sake — the only witch in
witchdom who isn't willing to scare you for her own
entertainment — ENJOY THEM ALL.
Yours ever,

Haggy Aggy

Your fantabulous shoe-loving friend,
Hagatha Agatha (Haggy Aggy for short, HA for shortest) xx

ISBN 9781846160653

ISBN 9781846160691

ISBN 9781846160721

ISBN 9781846160714

ISBN 9781846160677

ISBN 9781846160660

ISBN 9781846160707

ISBN 9781846160684